Tangled

The Junior Novelization

ISBN: 978-0-7364-2679-4

www.randomhouse.com/kids

Printed in the United States of America

10 9 8 7 6 5 4 3 2 1   First Edition

Tangled

The Junior Novelization

Adapted by Irene Trimble

Random House 🏠 New York

PROLOGUE

Once upon a time, a single drop of sunlight fell from the heavens. From it, a magical flower bloomed that had the power to heal the sick and frail.

One day, an old woman named Mother Gothel was singing softly to herself during one of her walks along a craggy hillside. She looked down and discovered the Golden Flower.

Just as she was about to pluck the flower from the ground, she noticed that it was glowing. As she kept singing, Mother Gothel's brittle voice became strong and clear. Her old bones didn't seem to ache anymore. She looked at her shriveled hand and saw that all her wrinkles were gone. Suddenly, she was young again, and her eyes widened with selfish delight!

Right then and there, Mother Gothel decided to leave the flower where it was, so that she could continue to use its power. It was a secret she kept all to herself. For centuries, she lived contentedly, singing to the flower each day, making it glow with the magic that kept her young and beautiful. And because of her covetous protection of the flower, no one else benefited from the blossom's healing gifts.

Over time, a small but happy kingdom flourished nearby. The beautiful kingdom was surrounded by sparkling blue water, its gentle waves dappled by sunlit skies, and the island itself was rich both in good fortune and in an easy harmony among its people. Though the people of the kingdom had heard the legend of the Golden Flower, no one had ever seen it. It was the stuff of stories told around fires on cold winter nights; the truth was, *they* had never really needed the flower.

The people of the kingdom had recently become especially joyful, as there was news that the Queen was to have a child. But all too soon, the kingdom's happiness came to an abrupt end. Word spread that the Queen was gravely ill. There seemed to be nothing that could help her.

Or was there? Perhaps the Golden Flower

was more than merely an old legend.

Willing to try anything to save her, the people launched a search throughout the kingdom and all the surrounding lands. They combed the hills and fields, mountains and valleys. They even crossed the clear blue water to explore the stark and rocky terrain on the opposite shore.

Mother Gothel, who had kept herself and the flower isolated from the people in the kingdom, was singing to the Golden Flower, as she did every day, when she spotted some strangers in the distance. They were searching every square inch of the land. *My flower!* Mother Gothel thought selfishly. *They mustn't find it. It belongs to me!* But Mother Gothel was wrong. The magical flower did not belong to her. And there was nothing she could do to stop others from benefiting from its healing powers.

Mother Gothel began to panic. Quickly, she hid and watched as the strangers moved closer to the rocky ledge where the Golden Flower grew.

"We found it! We found it!" the strangers shouted at last.

Mother Gothel watched, horrified, as a palace

guard uprooted the flower and carried it off. In a panic, she followed the strangers as they bore the precious flower to the castle. She stayed hidden, hoping to come up with a scheme to get the Golden Flower back.

But it was too late. The flower was made into a potion and fed to the ailing Queen. Its magic worked, and the Queen recovered! The King and all the people in the land rejoiced.

Soon afterward, the King and Queen stood on their royal balcony, holding the newborn Princess. She was a darling baby, with her mother's emerald-green eyes, and curly golden hair that gleamed in the sunlight. The palace courtyard was filled with the cheers of the kingdom's people as they saw their tiny princess for the first time.

But Mother Gothel, watching from the shadows, did not cheer. Without the magic of the Golden Flower, she was growing older by the day. Seething with anger, she waited.

As the day faded into night, the King and Queen launched a single glowing lantern into the night sky to celebrate their princess's birth.

All their love and hopes for the Princess's happiness were contained in the lantern. The crowd watched joyfully as the glowing lantern rose to the heavens.

But the King and Queen's happiness was short-lived. For later that night, as the kingdom slept, a vengeful Mother Gothel crept into the royal nursery and approached the Princess's cradle. Swiftly she thrust her hand toward the child—but suddenly stopped. The lovely golden curls of the infant entranced Mother Gothel. Compelled to gently stroke the baby's hair, she quietly began to sing, as she had done so many times with the flower.

Most unexpectedly, the child's hair began to glow! Mother Gothel watched in shock, then delight, as her withered old hand became young again. The healing power of the Golden Flower lived on in the golden hair of the little Princess!

Mother Gothel cut a piece of the Princess's hair and gazed at it as it lay in her hand. Now she could take it with her and use it anytime she liked.

But that was not to be. Mother Gothel

watched as the light hair in her hand turned dark brown. She looked at the back of the Princess's neck. There was a short brown tuft where the golden hair had been cut. Mother Gothel was furious! She realized that the magic only worked if she sang and stroked the hair on the Princess's head!

There was only one thing to do. She would have to steal the baby . . . and keep her hidden from the rest of the world forever.

Chapter 1

For many years the people of the kingdom searched and searched, but they never found their princess. No one knew that far away, hidden in a boxed-in valley, Mother Gothel was raising the child as her own. To prevent her from leaving, Mother Gothel kept the girl at the top of the tall tower they called home.

The beautiful valley provided stunning views for the little girl. A waterfall fell from the crest of the steep surrounding cliffs, plunging to a sparkling, winding stream below. The meadows were filled with flowers and lush greenery. Often rainbows rose from the water, glimmering and arching over the stone tower.

During the day, Mother Gothel would frequently go outside the tower to gather herbs and vegetables. On other occasions, the little girl watched as Mother Gothel went to the edge of the valley and slipped into a dark hole at the base of a rocky cliff, disappearing through a tunnel that led her beyond the places that the child could see.

The tunnel opened to a forest outside of the valley. Mother Gothel made sure that when she came and went through the tunnel, no one ever saw her. If anyone did see, they might find the hidden tower—and the Princess.

Mother Gothel adored Rapunzel. And the child loved Mother Gothel, too. After all, she was the only mother—the only person!—whom Rapunzel knew or remembered. Mother Gothel was there to feed and bathe the infant. She watched Rapunzel take her first steps. And she sang lullabies to the little girl as she stroked and brushed her hair every day. Rapunzel never knew the true love of her real parents.

Nearly four years passed before Rapunzel asked Mother Gothel, "Why can't I go outside?"

Mother Gothel remained cautious in her response. She knew she had to make the little girl fearful so she would never stray from the safety of the tower.

"The outside world is a dangerous place filled with horrible, selfish people," she replied. She did not want to lose Rapunzel. The child was a part of her now. She treasured Rapunzel as she would a prized rose or a precious jewel.

Mother Gothel lifted a section of Rapunzel's hair. Rapunzel reached back and touched the small tuft on the nape of her neck. It was the only part of her hair that was dark and short.

"They wanted your gift for themselves," Mother Gothel said, lying to Rapunzel as she gazed at the hair that she herself had cut. "So they cut a piece of your hair."

"Yes, Mommy." Rapunzel shivered a little. The outside world must be a terribly dangerous place.

But on the night of her fourth birthday, Rapunzel tiptoed over to the tower window. There in the night sky she saw thousands of sparkling lights drifting up beyond the ridge of the valley toward the stars.

The same thing happened on the night of

her fifth birthday, and on her sixth and seventh birthdays. Rapunzel loved those floating lights. She even grew to believe that somehow they were meant for her.

Rapunzel didn't know that each year, the King and Queen and all the people in the kingdom released thousands of glowing lanterns as beacons for their lost princess. They hoped that one day the lights would guide her home.

Years passed, and Rapunzel grew into a beautiful young woman with sparkling green eyes and golden hair that was nearly seventy feet long—seventy feet of hair that was used to make a swing so that she could swoop from the rafters in the tower, and that made brushes for her beloved paintings. And despite her lonely life spent inside the top of the tower, nothing could destroy Rapunzel's spirit.

With her eighteenth birthday approaching, Rapunzel had decided that this birthday would be different. At least, she hoped so. But first she had to gather enough courage to ask Mother

Gothel for the biggest favor she could grant. Mother Gothel had always told Rapunzel that someday, when she was old enough, when she was ready, she would be allowed to go outside. *Outside!* Rapunzel could only imagine outside—a place she barely glimpsed from her window, a place filled with creatures and plants and with sights, sounds, and smells she had never experienced!

Rapunzel nervously hoped that Mother Gothel would finally allow her to go out. She needed to find the source of those mysterious floating lights!

Chapter 2

Opening the tower's shutters, Rapunzel leaned out over the windowsill, breathing in the fresh morning air. It seemed to smell better out there than inside the tower, and the air always felt cooler and fresher at the window. From a potted strawberry plant next to her, a tiny green chameleon named Pascal came out to greet her. Pascal was Rapunzel's only friend, and he looked up at her happily, blinking his big eyes. He could turn almost any color. Now, sensing her mood, he turned a bright yellow.

Pascal knew, as always, exactly what was best for Rapunzel. She wanted to go outside! Pascal skittered over the windowsill and gestured for her to come out of the tower with him. But Rapunzel shook her head. She couldn't go out.

She needed Mother Gothel's permission. Pascal slumped a bit.

"Oh, come on, Pascal," she said cheerfully to the little chameleon as she motioned to him to come back inside the tower. "It's not that bad."

She used her golden hair to pull a lever. Thick wooden shutters that covered the windows over her head at the tower's peak burst open. The tower was flooded with sunlight, glittering specks of dust filling the air. Their day was about to begin—the day she would ask Mother Gothel to take her to see the sparkling lights!

The tower made a small living space—it was tall but narrow. On the main level, there was a small kitchen, along with a living room that had a giant fireplace. The window through which Mother Gothel entered and exited the tower was off to one side. Mother Gothel slept in a bedroom on this cozy level of the tower.

Up a set of winding wooden stairs was a small loft where Rapunzel slept. Here she also had a box of paints, a guitar, and a little bed for Pascal.

Rapunzel kept herself busy every day. But today Pascal felt her excitement as she rushed through her chores, cleaning, sweeping, dusting the furniture, waxing the floors made of thick golden wood and shining stone, and washing her single, pale purple dress. Then she sat down to play her guitar. She was self-taught, of course, but the melodies that floated from the strings were beautiful.

She had a few puzzles that she put together and took apart regularly. When she started feeling a bit pent up, she often turned to her darts. She had quite good aim and placed her targets in every nook and cranny to challenge herself with increasing levels of difficulty. Someday she might just create a dart that could fly across the valley and hit one of the far walls of the cliffs. But that day was a long way off. In the meantime, Rapunzel also loved to read! She had exactly three books, all completely memorized—one on culinary arts, which helped her with her cooking, one about geology; and the third about botany. Her favorite was the botany book. It had the best colors and explained about things that grew outside!

Pascal tried to be patient as Rapunzel

did the same things over and over again, but sometimes he couldn't help rolling his eyes. It was boring!—especially when she had to brush her hair for hours on end.

This morning, when she was finally done with all her chores, her guitar, her puzzles and books, her hair . . . Rapunzel smiled at Pascal. As usual, she had saved the best for last: painting! It was her passion. The tower's walls were covered with her art. Tossing a length of golden hair over one of the rafters, she hoisted herself up toward her favorite mural.

But today, as she pulled back the red curtain that covered the painting, she looked at it differently. The image was a replica of the view from her window—a night scene showing the glowing lights rising into the sky.

Pulling out her paints, she spotted a small blank space that she wanted to fill. When she finished, she had added a small picture of herself ready to enter the forest beyond the tunnel—to see the world outside her little valley.

Suddenly, Rapunzel heard her mother's voice. "Rapunzel!" Mother Gothel called from outside the tower. "Rapunzel! Let down your hair!"

Rapunzel gasped. The moment had finally arrived! She took a deep breath and turned to Pascal, who gave her a brave little smile.

Chapter 3

"Okay," Rapunzel said to Pascal, trying to be calm. "No big deal, I'm just going to do it. I'm just going to say, 'Mother? There's something I've been wanting to ask you!'" Rapunzel's strong voice grew faint as she added, "For eighteen years." She was beginning to feel her heart sinking. Maybe she wasn't ready to go outside.

Pascal took one look at Rapunzel and arched his little body, puffing out his chest to tell her to be brave.

"I know, Pascal," Rapunzel said, appreciating the encouragement. "Come on, now," she said, motioning to him to hide. "Don't let her see you." Mother Gothel had never approved of indoor pets.

Pascal nodded and camouflaged himself to look like the stone on the mantel.

Down below, Mother Gothel yelled, "Rapunzel! I'm not getting any younger down here!" Rapunzel hurried toward the window.

"Coming, Mother!" Rapunzel shouted. She placed a loop of her golden hair around a pulley outside the window and lowered it down. As soon as Mother Gothel set her foot in the loop of hair, Rapunzel began to pull her slowly up to the tower window. It was hard work!

"Hello, Mother!" Rapunzel said, nearly out of breath.

"Rapunzel, how do you manage to do that every day? It looks absolutely exhausting!" Mother Gothel said as she climbed inside.

"Oh, it's nothing," Rapunzel replied cheerfully.

"Then I don't know why it takes so long," Mother Gothel snapped, adding in the sweetest voice she could muster, "Oh, I'm just teasing."

Meanwhile, Rapunzel remained focused on her big question.

"Uh, so, Mother—" she began. But Mother

Gothel immediately interrupted her.

"Oh, Rapunzel, look in the mirror. Do you know what I see?" she said, pulling Rapunzel into a half hug as they stood side by side. "I see a strong, confident, beautiful young lady."

Rapunzel was puzzled, until she realized Mother Gothel was talking about her own reflection!

Rapunzel took a breath and tried to speak to her mother again.

"So . . . Mother?" Rapunzel began, stumbling nervously over her words. "As you know, tomorrow I turn eighteen. And I wanted to ask . . . what I really want for this birthday . . . actually, I've wanted it for quite a few birthdays now . . ."

Mother Gothel shook her head impatiently. "Oh, Rapunzel, please stop with the mumbling. You know how I feel about the mumbling. 'Blah blah blah!' It's very annoying."

Rapunzel sighed. Pascal made a gesture for Rapunzel to keep going.

Rapunzel nodded and blurted out, "I want to see the floating lights!"

Mother Gothel was stunned. Rapunzel herself was stunned. *I did it!* she thought. *I finally asked!*

"What?" Mother Gothel said to Rapunzel.

"Well," Rapunzel answered, "I was hoping you would take me to see the floating lights this year."

"Oh, you mean the stars," Mother Gothel said, hoping Rapunzel was still young enough to be fooled.

Rapunzel shook her head. "That's the thing," she said excitedly, "I've charted stars and they're always constant. But these? They appear every year on my birthday, Mother! Only on my birthday! And I can't help but feel that they're meant for me!

"I need to see them, Mother," she said. "And not just from my window—in person. I have to know what they are."

Mother Gothel tried to appear calm. "Go outside?" she said as she gathered her wits. "Why, Rapunzel, you know why we stay up in this tower."

"I know," Rapunzel replied. A shiver crept up

her back as Mother Gothel described terrible, frightening things—men, ruffians and thugs, with sharp fangs and weapons.

Mother Gothel kept going until she felt certain Rapunzel understood that she was responsible for protecting her gift: her magical golden hair. Then she spoke firmly: "Rapunzel. Don't ever ask to leave this tower again."

"Yes, Mother," Rapunzel replied obediently, slumping in sadness.

"Oh . . ." Mother Gothel changed her tone and swept Rapunzel into a warm hug. "I love you very much, dear."

"I love you more," Rapunzel answered quietly, as she always did.

"I love you most!" Mother Gothel whispered as she kissed Rapunzel atop her head and got ready to leave again.

Rapunzel looked up at the sky. How could she doubt her mother's love? She looked down and waved as Mother Gothel disappeared beyond the walls of the valley . . . into the mysterious world beyond.

Chapter 4

At that very moment, a dashing thief named Flynn Rider was running through the forest as fast as he could. The two Stabbington brothers, his partners in crime, ran with him.

Hot on their heels rode the mounted palace guards. The guards' highly trained and powerful white horses were as intent on catching the thieves as the guards themselves. Flynn Rider and the Stabbington brothers had stolen the crown that belonged to the long-lost princess. In the kingdom, this was no joking matter. The people still believed that their princess would return one day, and her crown must be ready for her! The royal guards would stop at nothing to get it back.

Flynn Rider halted at a tree and tried to

catch his breath. Noticing a WANTED poster of himself, he scoffed, "Would you look at this?" The Stabbington brothers stared blankly at the poster. "Is it too much to ask to get my nose right?" Flynn felt insulted. "It's just so . . . bulbous," he added petulantly.

"There they are!" A group of the royal guards had spotted the thieves from a ridge above. Flynn stuffed the poster into his satchel as he and the Stabbingtons took off. Again they ran at top speed, but they soon found themselves trapped at the end of a ravine. The only way out was to climb the sheer fifteen-foot walls.

Though the burly Stabbington brothers were Flynn's partners, they were probably the most dangerous cutthroats he had ever met. They were identical twins, big and strong, with matching scars. The only way Flynn could tell them apart was that one of them wore an eye patch and never spoke. But right now Flynn was worried that they might kill him for the crown. He needed a plan to escape them and the royal guards!

"Okay," Flynn said, thinking fast, "give me a

boost and then I'll pull you up."

"Give us the satchel first," demanded the brother without the eye patch.

"What?" Flynn pretended to be stunned, hurt! "Why, I just can't believe that after all we've been through together, you don't trust me!"

But the Stabbington brothers wouldn't budge. Flynn could see that it was hopeless. Grumbling, he handed the brothers the satchel containing the crown and began climbing over their shoulders. But Flynn was a clever fellow. As he climbed, he grabbed the satchel back, unnoticed.

When he reached the top of the ledge, he held up the satchel and gave the brothers a grin.

"Enjoy prison!" he called back as he ran away. "Find a hobby!"

The captain of the royal guard saw Flynn making a run for it. "He's getting away!" he shouted. "Don't let him get away!"

A shower of arrows rained down around Flynn, but he dodged them all, leaping over rocks and fallen trees, skirting bushes, and ducking under low-hanging branches.

With the royal guards still hot on his trail, Flynn spotted a Y-shaped tree up ahead and ran right for it. He hurled himself straight though the opening in the Y, landing safely on the other side. The horses of the royal guard stumbled to a stop behind him—all but one. The captain's horse! Flynn was astounded.

"Ha! We've got him now, Maximus!" the captain said to his muscle-bound white horse. "He won't get away this time!" Flynn took a quick glance back at the horse. How had he jumped through that gap?

Grabbing a vine, Flynn swung through the air and looped back, knocking the captain right off his horse and taking his place in the saddle.

"Hee-yah!" Flynn yelled triumphantly, feeling pretty smug. He knew he'd pulled off a classic move. But his grin quickly left his face when the horse suddenly came to a halt, nearly throwing Flynn out of the saddle.

"Come on, Fleabag!" Flynn yelled.

Maximus was the best horse in the kingdom, and he did not like being called Fleabag. The horse whipped his head around angrily and started nipping at Flynn's precious satchel.

"No!" Flynn shouted. "Stop it! Stop it! Bad horse, bad horse!"

Maximus began spinning in circles, trying to throw Flynn, but the young thief held on tightly.

"Whoa, who-o-o-o-oah!" Flynn shouted. Flynn had a new enemy—a maniacal horse!

Chapter 5

"**G**ive me that!" Flynn yelled as Maximus finally sank his teeth into the satchel. Man and horse engaged in a tug-of-war until Flynn used all his might to pull the satchel free, flinging it well out of reach. It landed at the far end of a fallen tree that was rooted in the side of the cliff and stretched across the top of the deep ravine.

Panting, Flynn and Maximus immediately sized up the situation. Not used to having such a competent rival, Flynn leaped from the horse's back and scrambled to get to the tree first. Maximus followed. Flynn grinned as he slipped along the underside of the tree and inched toward the satchel. No horse would dare step out on a tree overhanging a cliff.

No horse except Maximus.

The horse walked out onto the tree, trying to stomp on Flynn's hands with his hooves. Flynn could not believe it. The massive horse was practically tiptoeing along the top of the horizontal tree.

"Ha-ha!" Flynn yelled at last. Triumphantly, he clung to the end of the tree, hanging on to a branch that simply could not hold the horse's weight. Flynn held up the satchel to show Maximus that he had won.

Maximus glared at Flynn.

Crack! Now they both froze as they heard the deep sound of the tree roots pulling away from the ledge. Flynn and Maximus fell, screaming and neighing, as the tree broke from the cliff.

Maximus landed hard. Quickly, he got to his feet and shook off the dust. He was all right! But Flynn was nowhere to be found. The horse sniffed around, trying to pick up Flynn's trail.

Carefully and quietly, Flynn moved along a steep rocky wall. He had the satchel. He had the crown. Now he just had to get rid of that crazy horse! Seeing some bushes, he plunged his hand into them and parted their branches. He peered into the darkness and saw a cave. Perfect! He slipped into the entrance just as Maximus trotted by, sniffing like a bloodhound.

That horse is relentless! Flynn thought as he held his breath. Turning, he saw that the cave had an opening on the opposite side. He was so desperate to get away from the horse that he plunged farther inside without a second's thought, and found himself in a tunnel. When he emerged from the tunnel, he stopped short.

Before him lay a beautiful valley. The ground was covered in lush green foliage. A waterfall glimmered in the sunlight as it tumbled down the rusty-red, rocky walls surrounding the valley and splashed into a clean, fresh pond. A sparkling bright blue stream burbled along a winding path amid fields of flowers.

And in the middle of the valley, a tall tower reached toward the sky. Stunned by the valley's beauty and awed by this hidden world, Flynn simply stared for a moment. He had discovered something truly marvelous.

Flynn could faintly hear Maximus at the

far end of the tunnel. Groaning, Flynn realized that he had to do something fast to get away— something that Maximus would never be able to do. Flynn raced to the tower. He pulled out some arrows and used them to hoist himself up. It was a grueling effort, but he had to find refuge. Grimacing all the way, Flynn plunged arrow after arrow into the cracks in the tower's exterior, pulling himself ever higher.

Moments later, Flynn climbed through the window at the top of the tower.

"Alone at last," he said, heaving a sigh of relief. He had finally found a safe harbor where no royal guard or royal horse or Stabbington brother would ever find him.

BANG! Something hit Flynn in the back of the head. Then his world went black.

Chapter 6

Rapunzel stood over Flynn's unconscious body. She was still marveling at the power of a frying pan against the first real person she had ever seen besides Mother Gothel. *He must be a ruffian,* she thought. Mother Gothel had warned her about ruffians.

When Rapunzel realized she'd knocked the man out, she began looking at his hands. She poked at him with the pan and then used it to turn him over. She examined his eyes and peeled back his lips to check for fangs.

But there were no pointy teeth. This ruffian actually looked rather nice.

She turned to Pascal. Now what should she do with the ruffian? But Pascal just shrugged, not knowing what color to turn.

Rapunzel started to shiver all over. She had just overpowered an evil man—someone who must have come in search of her golden hair.

The man groaned, and Rapunzel leaped back. She had to do something with him before he awoke, maybe lock him up in a place from which he could never escape! She took his arms and dragged him across the room. He was heavier than Mother Gothel! Spotting the closet, she knew she had found the right place to put him. He would never be able to escape the closet! Bending and twisting his body, she pushed him inside, then slammed the doors. She wedged a chair in front of the doors to keep them closed.

"Okay, okay," she said to herself, "I've got a person in my closet." *Wait.* That meant— "I've got a person in my closet!" Rapunzel was beside herself. She had conquered an evil, terrible monster and locked him away! "I've got a person in my closet!" she repeated frantically.

Her worry suddenly turned to excitement. "I've got a person in my closet!" she exclaimed happily to Pascal. This was proof that she could handle anything. She was ready! Mother Gothel would see that she could handle a person and go outside! She could go to see the lanterns!

Rapunzel noticed a satchel on the floor. The jeweled crown was sticking out. Rapunzel had no idea what it was. To her, it looked like a giant ring. She pulled it out and inspected it. She put it on her wrist. Pascal took one look and shook his head. This thing was much too big to be a bracelet.

Rapunzel was puzzled. The thing was shiny, but it was not a ring or a bracelet. Maybe it was a necklace! But as she lifted it to put it around her neck, she felt it nestle neatly atop her hair. It was a hat!

Rapunzel went to the mirror to see what the thing looked like on her head.

But . . . there was something odd about the thing. It fit snugly and felt like something that belonged on her head. Her eyes sparkled. The reflection in the mirror triggered a funny feeling deep inside. Who was that person looking at her from the mirror? Who was she?

Suddenly a voice came from outside the

tower. "Rapunzel! Let down your hair!"

It was Mother Gothel. "Uh, one moment, Mother!" Rapunzel called back. Quickly she tossed the crown and the satchel into a pot.

"I have a surprise!" Mother Gothel shouted cheerfully.

"I do, too!" Rapunzel answered as she let down her hair.

"Oh, I bet my surprise is bigger!"

As Rapunzel started pulling her mother up the side of the tower, she glanced at the closet and whispered to herself, "I seriously doubt it."

"I brought back parsnips!" Mother Gothel announced as soon as she reached the windowsill. "And I'm going to make hazelnut soup for dinner. Your favorite! Surprise!"

But Rapunzel was not all that surprised or excited about the parsnips and the hazelnut soup. No, Rapunzel was bursting at the seams to talk to Mother Gothel about her quest to see the floating lanterns. She had found the perfect solution: a ruffian who could serve as a guide!

Chapter 7

"Well, Mother, there's something I want to tell you," Rapunzel said cautiously. Mother Gothel started to ramble about their earlier argument, telling Rapunzel that she was wrong and Mother Gothel was right. But Rapunzel remained focused.

"Okay," she said. "I've been thinking a lot about what you said earlier, and—"

"I hope you're not still talking about the stars," Mother Gothel said impatiently.

"Floating lights," Rapunzel said quickly, "and yes . . . I'm leading up to that, but—"

"Because I really thought we dropped the issue, sweetheart."

"No, Mother," Rapunzel said. She needed to say that she had captured a ruffian—all by herself! "I'm just saying, you think I'm not strong enough to handle myself out there, but—"

Mother Gothel laughed. "Oh, darling, *I know* you're not strong enough to handle yourself out there."

"But if you'd just listen . . . ," Rapunzel said, not wanting to quarrel with her, but definitely wanting her to stop talking and pay attention.

"Rapunzel, we're done talking about this," Mother Gothel snapped.

"Trust me," Rapunzel said, determined to go on with what she had to say.

"Rapunzel—" Mother Gothel was warning her.

"I know what I'm—"

"Rapunzel!" Mother Gothel shouted. "ENOUGH WITH THE LIGHTS, RAPUNZEL! YOU ARE NOT LEAVING THIS TOWER! EVER!"

Mother Gothel stood in the center of the room, her fists clenched at her sides. Rapunzel was dumbfounded. All at once she realized that it didn't matter what she did or said. There was no hope that Mother Gothel would ever let her go outside. Rapunzel would be trapped at the top of the tower for the rest of her life.

Rapunzel turned and looked longingly at her mural of lights, then at her closet. Inside that closet was proof that she could handle herself in the outside world. Inside that closet was a ruffian whom she had captured. By herself!

Inside that closet was the guide who would take her to see the sparkling lights. Mother Gothel would never have to know about it.

Rapunzel made her decision.

"All I was going to say, Mother, is that I know what I want for my birthday now."

"And what is that?" Mother Gothel asked.

"New paint," Rapunzel answered. "The paint made from the white shells you once brought me."

"Well, that's a very long trip, Rapunzel. Almost three days' time," Mother Gothel said, shaking her head, trying to dissuade Rapunzel.

But this time, Rapunzel replied in kind. This time, everything was different. This time, Rapunzel knew what she wanted, and she knew exactly how to get it.

"I just thought it was a better idea than the stars."

Mother Gothel's face brightened a bit. This was what she wanted to hear. "You'll be all right on your own?"

"I know I'm safe as long as I'm here," Rapunzel answered.

Mother Gothel sighed. She got up, packed some food for her journey, and kissed Rapunzel on the top of the head. "All right, then. I'll be back in three days' time," she said. "I love you very much, dear."

"I love you more!" Rapunzel said brightly, and then began helping Mother Gothel down the tower.

"I love you most," Mother Gothel called back.

Rapunzel watched from her window until Mother Gothel disappeared into the forest. Then, using her hair, she pulled the closet doors open.

The man in the closet was still unconscious. Quickly, Rapunzel sat him on a chair. Then she firmly tied him up with her hair.

Rapunzel leaped up to the rafters, held up her pan, and waited, ready for anything. Pascal jumped on the man and tried waking him by slapping his face with his little tail. No response. Pascal looked at Rapunzel. She urged him on. Pascal slapped his tail against the man's cheek again. Still no response.

Pascal thought for a moment. Then he slipped his long tongue into the man's ear.

"Blll-AHH!" Flynn awoke abruptly. Pascal's tongue was gross and—and it tickled!

"Struggling is pointless," Rapunzel said firmly. Then she jumped down from the rafters and faced him.

Chapter 8

"I know what you're here for," Rapunzel continued, brandishing her pan, "and I'm not afraid of you."

"What?" Flynn answered, confused by it all. Who was this young woman with the hair that seemed to fill the room?

"Who are you and how did you find me?" Rapunzel asked him.

Flynn hesitated, and Rapunzel raised her pan. "Okay, okay, all right," he said quickly, not wanting to be hit on the head again.

Flynn was now getting a better view of this young woman. She had striking green eyes, and her hair, though excessive, was a beautiful shining gold. *She* was beautiful. But what did she want from him?

Flynn tried to be charming. "I know not who you are, nor how I came to find you, but may I just say . . . ? Hi." Flynn raised an eyebrow and gave Rapunzel a devilish grin. "The name's Flynn Rider. How's your day going?"

Rapunzel had no idea what the man was trying to do, but he looked really weird. Maybe he was insane! "Who else knows my location, Flynn Rider?" Rapunzel demanded. She needed to know everything before she proceeded with her plan.

Flynn sighed. "I was . . . in a situation, gallivanting through the forest. I came across your tower, and—" Flynn stopped short, filled with alarm. "Where is my satchel?"

"I've hidden it somewhere you'll never find it," Rapunzel said confidently.

But it only took about two seconds, during which he surveyed the room and glanced at Rapunzel, for Flynn to say: "It's in that pot, isn't it?"

How did he know? Rapunzel raised the pan. *BANG!* She hit him again. Rapunzel looked at the unconscious man and wondered if maybe she had overreacted just a bit. That pan seemed to be a very good weapon for knocking out ruffians. Quickly, she looked around to hide the satchel again, somewhere really good this time. She lifted a loose board in the stairs and stashed the satchel underneath.

A few minutes later, Pascal flicked his tongue into Flynn's ear again and Flynn woke with a jump. "Would you stop that!" Flynn yelled, squirming.

Rapunzel just smiled and said, "Now it's hidden where you'll never find it."

She paced around him, wrapping him ever more tightly in her long hair. She was definitely feeling more confident, knowing the power of the pan. "So, what do you want with my hair? To cut it?" she asked accusingly." To sell it?"

"No! Listen, the only thing I want to do with your hair is get out of it," Flynn said. "Literally."

"Wait. You don't want my hair?" Rapunzel asked in disbelief. Mother Gothel had always said that everyone would want to steal it.

"Why on earth would I want your hair?" Flynn asked. "Look, I was being chased, I saw a tower, and I climbed it. End of story."

Rapunzel eyed him. If he didn't want her hair, then she could trust him! Bracing herself, she got ready to take the next step in her plan.

"Okay, Flynn Rider," she said finally. "I'm prepared to offer you a deal."

"Deal?" Flynn said, willing to listen.

"Look this way," she told him. Rapunzel headed toward the fireplace, her hair still wrapped around Flynn. His chair twirled like a spinning top.

"Do you know what these are?" she asked, stepping up on the mantel above the fireplace. She pulled back the curtain, revealing the mural of the floating lights.

Flynn nodded. "You mean the lantern thing they do for the Princess?"

"Lanterns?" Rapunzel gasped quietly. "I knew they weren't stars!"

Chapter 9

More confident than ever before, Rapunzel presented her plan to Flynn: "Well, tomorrow night, they will light the night sky with these lanterns. You will act as my guide, take me to the castle, and return me home safely. Then and only then will I return your satchel to you. That is my deal."

Flynn refused.

Pascal punched his fist to give Rapunzel courage. Standing tall atop the mantel, her frying pan in hand, she said in her strongest voice, "You can tear this tower apart brick by brick. But without my help, you will never find your precious satchel."

Flynn repeated the offer Rapunzel had made: "I take you to see the lanterns, bring you back home, and you'll give me back my satchel?"

Rapunzel nodded, adding, "I promise. And when I promise something, I never, ever break that promise. Ever."

But Flynn knew he could not go to the kingdom—not now! He was a wanted thief. So he changed his strategy. He relied on his charm and good looks. Confidently he pursed his lips and oh-so-carefully raised one eyebrow. He knew this was his handsomest expression.

Nothing happened. Flynn waited for Rapunzel to react.

Rapunzel waited for something to happen. Having never been with other people, she had no idea what this Flynn Rider was doing, but he did look awfully strange. It was kind of like that crazy look he had given her earlier.

"This is kind of an off day for me," Flynn said, beginning to doubt himself. He was finding it hard to believe that this young woman was not swept off her feet by his charms!

"Fine," Flynn said finally, "I'll take you to see the lanterns."

"Really?" Rapunzel exclaimed. This. Was.

It! She was going to see the lights! She was so excited, she began jumping about the room, leaving Flynn bouncing in his hair-bound position on the chair, landing, at last, facedown on the floor.

A little while later, Flynn, unbound and freed from Rapunzel's hair, began to climb down the tower the same way he had come up, using his arrows. He could not believe he was actually leaving this place. Just a while ago, he had thought it would be a place to hide from that horse!

Halfway down, he looked up. Rapunzel was standing in the window. She was still holding her pan in case of any trouble. She hadn't moved an inch.

"You coming?" Flynn shouted up at her.

Rapunzel arranged her hair to let herself down from the tower safely. Then she checked to make sure Pascal had securely tied himself in her hair. The little chameleon gave her a thumbs-up for courage. This was her big day! She was terrified.

Turning, she looked back at her mural and

stared at the lights she'd had painted on her wall for so many years. She'd been drawn to the lights all her life, and now, if she had the courage, she'd get to see them. She wished Mother Gothel had agreed to take her, but she knew she'd have to do this for herself.

Slowly, she climbed down the tower for the first time. Using her hair like a rope—as she had done so many times for Mother Gothel, but never for herself—she rappelled toward the ground. At the bottom of the tower, her toes touched the soft grass. Then she was standing on the ground for the first time in her life! The grass tickled her toes. It was cool. It felt wonderful. The sky looked enormous. The sunlight shimmered through the trees. It smelled fresh. Outside was great!

"Woo-hoo!" Rapunzel shouted, dancing in the sunlight. "I can't believe I did this! I can't believe I did this!"

Pascal hung on for dear life.

Chapter 10

"This is incredible!" Rapunzel said as she and Flynn walked deeper into the forest. But then she remembered how her mother would feel if she knew she'd disobeyed her. Rapunzel shook her head. "Mother would be so furious." She looked at Flynn and said, "But it's okay. I mean, what she doesn't know won't kill her, right?" Flynn just shrugged and nodded.

Rapunzel knelt down to look at some leaves and mud on the forest floor. Everything was new and beautiful to her. She'd never seen anything like it.

"This is so fun!" she said to Flynn.

Rapunzel climbed a tree, and ran through a field of flowers. Then she saw a hill. A big, grassy hill. It looked . . . fun! She threw herself on her back and rolled down the hill, filled with delight. She wrapped her hair around a branch and swung through the air, hollering, "Best! Day! Ever!"

Finally, remembering Mother Gothel again, she slumped against a boulder and sobbed.

Flynn sat down next to her. "You know," he said gently, "I can't help but notice . . . you seem a little at war with yourself here."

"What?" Rapunzel asked feebly.

Flynn moved closer, trying to seem gentle. He had an idea. He would play on Rapunzel's guilt to force her to take him back to the tower, where he could retrieve his satchel and go on with his life!

"I'm just picking up bits and pieces," he said to her softly, in a sugary-sweet voice. "Overprotective mother. Forbidden road trip. I mean, this is serious stuff. But let me ease your conscience: this is part of growing up. A little rebellion, a little adventure, that's good! Healthy, even!"

"You think?" Rapunzel perked up a little.

"I know!" Flynn said confidently. "You're

way overthinking this. Trust me. Does your mother deserve it? No. Would this break her heart and crush her soul? Of course. But you've just got to do it!"

"She would be heartbroken," Rapunzel concluded.

Flynn tried to look as distressed as Rapunzel. He had her wrapped around his little finger! He said as gently as he could, helping her to her feet, "Oh, bother. All right, I can't believe I'm saying this, but—I'm letting you out of the deal."

"What?" Rapunzel said. She knew she probably should go back to Mother Gothel, but she liked it outside. Nobody had hurt her. Maybe Mother Gothel had just been wrong about some things.

Flynn started to lead her back toward the tower. "Don't thank me," he was saying. "Let's just get you home. I get back my satchel, you get back a mother-daughter relationship based on mutual trust, and *voilà!*—we part ways as unlikely friends."

Rapunzel pulled herself together. She wasn't

ready to go back to the tower. "No. No," she said firmly. "I'm seeing those lanterns."

"Oh, c'mon!" Flynn whined. "What is it going to take for me to get my satchel back?"

Just then, something rustled through the bushes. "What is it?" Rapunzel asked, terrified. "Is it ruffians? Thugs? Have they come for me?" She leaped behind Flynn for protection.

A fuzzy rabbit jumped out of the bushes. Rapunzel blushed. *Okay, now, that was a little embarrassing.* She wondered if Flynn noticed that she had overreacted a bit.

"Probably be best if we avoid ruffians and thugs?" Flynn asked.

Rapunzel agreed, "That'd probably be best."

Flynn suddenly had an idea. "Are you hungry?" he said with a devious smile, still determined to scare her back to the tower—and his precious satchel with the crown. "I know a great place for lunch."

"Where?" Rapunzel asked.

"Oh, don't worry," Flynn told her, grinning. "You'll know it when you smell it."

Chapter 11

In another part of the forest, Maximus, the palace guard horse, was still eagerly sniffing the ground for Flynn Rider. Furious about losing Flynn, he saw one of Flynn's WANTED posters. In a frenzy, Maximus ripped it from the tree with his teeth and shredded it into tiny bits. Maximus was not used to failing in a chase. And he definitely was not going to fail in this one. He had nothing but disdain for that cocky thief, and he couldn't stand the thought that the man had evaded him. Maximus knew that he was considered the best horse in the royal guard. He had helped his humans win awards, promotions, and bonuses. And all that he asked for in return was a warm stable, some hay, and maybe a few oats every day.

But this was different. When it came to this conniving, disrespectful thief, Maximus had reached his limit. He wanted to apprehend Flynn Rider himself!

Maximus sniffed the air, trying to pick up the scoundrel's scent. He looked for the puny footprints left by the puny man who barely made an imprint in the soil. Maximus knew—he knew—he would find those prints, however small, and track down Flynn Rider.

Suddenly, his ears perked up. There was a rustling in the bushes. Aha! The horse hid behind a large green bush, ready to catch that man. A figure, dark and shadowy, approached. When the figure got just close enough, he leaped out to confront it. But it wasn't Flynn he found. He was face to face with Mother Gothel!

Who is she? Maximus wondered.

Mother Gothel was wondering the same thing about the horse. Startled at first, she quickly noticed the kingdom's emblem on the horse's bridle.

"A palace horse?" she mumbled to herself. "Where is your rider?" The palace guards rarely came around this area of the forest, not since—

"Oh, no," Mother Gothel gasped. "Rapunzel!" There was no other explanation. The horse's rider must have been searching for Rapunzel. That was the only reason for any royal guard to be in this part of the forest. What if he had found the tunnel into the valley, leaving the horse outside?

In a panic, Mother Gothel turned and ran back toward the tower. When she got there, she called out, "Rapunzel? Rapunzel! Let down your hair!" But no one answered.

She ran to the back of the tower. Long ago, she had used this entrance. But once Rapunzel's hair had grown long enough for Mother Gothel to use it as a way of entering and exiting the tower, she had closed off the door, with bricks and mortar. Now, she ripped at the branches that had grown over the door and uncovered the hidden entrance.

At least no one got in this way, she thought as she began prying away the bricks with her bare hands, until she could open the door behind the wall she had built.

Climbing a secret staircase, Mother Gothel burst through a door hidden in the floor. She looked around the tower. It was just as she feared. The tower was empty.

In a fury, Mother Gothel ransacked the tower. Rapunzel couldn't leave. She had raised the child! Rapunzel believed everything Mother Gothel had told her. All that work nurturing her precious flower, the child with the magical hair—had it all been for naught?

"Rapunzel!" she called out desperately. Then she saw a glint of something under the stairs. She moved toward it, walking up a few steps, and a board creaked under her foot.

Mother Gothel ripped the board away and found a satchel hidden underneath. She pulled it out and looked inside. Much to her horror, she found a crown inside. The crown of the lost princess! Then she saw the WANTED poster with Flynn Rider's picture on it.

Mother Gothel wasted no time. She grabbed a dagger and the satchel and quickly left the empty tower.

Chapter 12

As Mother Gothel tore through the forest searching for Rapunzel, Flynn and Rapunzel were still searching for a place to eat.

"Ah, there it is!" Flynn exclaimed at last. "The Snuggly Duckling!"

Rapunzel stared at the little tavern. It looked interesting. She cocked her head. The crooked old wooden building was tucked into the base of a large tree. It seemed as if the tree and the building had grown together and the tree had determined which way they would grow. Having never seen any building other than the stone tower, she thought it seemed perfectly natural that the wooden shingles and shutters would fit right into the tree. One wall of the tavern bent out around a root. The peak of the tavern's roof curved down under a limb. And the tavern seemed wobbly all over.

Outside the tavern, there were some horses. They seemed gentle. She wasn't too frightened of them, but she did wonder why they were tied to a fence.

"Don't worry," Flynn said. "It's a very quaint place, perfect for you. Don't want you getting scared and giving up on this whole endeavor, now, do we?"

He was determined to terrify that girl right back to her tower, retrieve his crown, and cash it in.

"Well, I do like ducklings," Rapunzel said, trying to be positive as she worried about the possibility of finding ruffians inside.

"Who doesn't?" Flynn said brightly. "I'm buying. And by buying," he said with a wink, "I mean stealing. And by stealing, I mean taking unlawfully." He chuckled to himself. This girl was oh, so naïve! She was practically clinging to him, her body trembling in fear.

"Garçon!" Flynn shouted to the greasy tavern keeper as they entered the ramshackle establishment. "Your finest table, please!"

The tavern was dark and musty inside. It was noisy, too, filled with the sounds of men yelling and fighting, laughing and grumbling. Rapunzel's eyes widened. A silence fell over the room as she and Flynn entered. When her eyes adjusted to the gloom, she looked around. The tavern was filled with a large group of terrifying, brutish men!

Ruffians and thugs! Rapunzel's heart raced. *They want my hair!*

Rapunzel was horrified as she and Flynn made their way through the tavern. The thugs were battle-scarred and wore armor that had been pierced by arrows; they carried axes and spears. Not a single one had bathed or shaved. Poor Pascal turned sickly green when he saw that the cook was making lizard stew.

Suddenly, Rapunzel felt someone grab a piece of her hair.

"That's a lot of hair," the thug said menacingly.

"Is that blood in your mustache?" Flynn asked another, smaller thug. "Look at this, look at all the blood in his mustache!" Flynn said to Rapunzel.

Rapunzel backed away in terror and bumped into another thug. "Sorry," she said to the man. "Sorry."

Flynn could see that Rapunzel was as white as a ghost. His plan was working. "Hey, you don't look so good, Blondie. Maybe we should get you home, call it a day?" he suggested hopefully.

"Okay." Rapunzel nodded.

"Probably better off doing just that." Flynn shrugged. "This is a five-star joint, after all. And if you can't handle this place, well, maybe you should be back in your tower."

Flynn had opened the door to leave when a huge hand grabbed the door and slammed it. The hand slapped the WANTED poster of Flynn onto the door.

"Is this you?" the huge man said.

Now Flynn turned pale. He was in a room full of thugs, and his experience with thugs was that they didn't show much mercy when a reward was involved.

Chapter 13

Every thug in the room eyed the reward mentioned on the poster. All heads turned in Flynn's direction with a keen interest.

"It's him, all right," one thug said. "Greno, go find some guards."

"That reward's gonna buy me a new hook," a one-armed thug said, licking his chops.

The bartender grabbed Flynn. "I could use the money," he said.

"What about me?" another thug interrupted. "I'm broke."

A brawl quickly ensued, with bottles crashing and chairs flying. Everyone was pulling at Flynn. Pascal and Rapunzel ducked and cringed, terrified.

"Please!" Flynn squealed from under the pile

Rapunzel grows up in a hidden tower.

The thief Flynn Rider thinks he's more handsome
than the picture on his WANTED poster.

The palace horse Maximus relentlessly pursues Flynn.

The Stabbington brothers are Flynn's
cutthroat partners in crime.

Pascal the chameleon gives Rapunzel
encouragement to face Flynn.

Rapunzel is surprised to finally
see Flynn Rider up close.

Rapunzel easily ties up Flynn with her hair.

Flynn tries to win over Rapunzel with
his charming good looks. It doesn't work.

Rapunzel joyfully rappels down from
the tower for the first time ever!

Rapunzel's adventures bring her true spirit to light.

of filthy men. "We can work this out!" But the only replies were grunts, shouts, and growls.

Rapunzel tried to help. She raised her frying pan and spoke up. "Um, excuse me? Ruffians?" she said.

"Gentlemen! Please!" Flynn cried as one of his arms was twisted behind his back and his knee was jammed into a table.

"Is it possible to just get my guide back?" Rapunzel shouted. She poked one of the thugs with her pan. "Just stop. Stop!" Nothing happened.

Rapunzel looked around. She saw a large table and jumped on top of it. It was time to take action! She whacked her pan against a giant pot hanging from the ceiling. *CLANG!* Then, with all her might, she yelled, "PUT HIM DOWN!"

For a moment, there was absolute silence. Every thug in the tavern stopped what he was doing and stared at the young woman.

Rapunzel took a breath. "Okay," she said to the rabid mob, "I don't know where I am, and I need him to take me to see the lanterns because

I've been dreaming about them my entire life! Find your humanity!" she pleaded. "Haven't you ever had a dream?"

Flynn cringed. A dream? Did she really want to talk about dreams with this crowd? His heart sank. He was definitely going to end up with a broken nose.

Then the thug with a hook for a hand moved toward Rapunzel with a menacing look. Rapunzel froze.

"I had a dream once," the brute said softly. He tossed aside his axe and told Rapunzel that he'd dreamed of being a pianist. Finding a small piano, he began to play.

A burly thug covered in bumps and bruises took the opportunity to tell Rapunzel about his dream. He handed her a flower. He wanted to fall in love! Rapunzel patted his hand.

Flynn was becoming more and more interested. What was up with this young woman, anyway? He watched as the tavern thugs turned to mush, weeping and sweetly telling Rapunzel about their dreams. They confessed to wanting to become everything from florists to ballet dancers. And all the while, her faithful chameleon, Pascal, sat on her shoulder, protectively looking out for her. Everyone seemed to adore her!

Unfortunately, something terribly serious was happening outside.

Mother Gothel had tracked Rapunzel and Flynn to the Snuggly Duckling. When she looked through the window, she was stunned. Rapunzel was happily mingling with those thugs! Mother Gothel felt her world crumbling around her. Without Rapunzel locked away in that tower—without the girl's magical hair—Mother Gothel's life would come to an abrupt end as she quickly aged. She had to do something to stop the naïve girl!

Inside, the crowd finally turned to Flynn Rider. "What about you?" the man with the hook for a hand asked. "What's your dream?"

Desperately hoping his answer would be enough, Flynn told them about his dream of living on his own island. The thugs roared their approval and tossed Flynn in the air.

"I have one, too!" Rapunzel shouted. She

knew she could trust these men with her dream. "I want to see the floating lanterns more than anything in the world!" She described how wonderful it felt—to her surprise—to be outside the tower. She was learning more and more with each passing minute, and she loved the sights she was seeing, the sounds she was hearing, and the people she was meeting.

The thugs cheered.

Outside, spying through the window, Mother Gothel controlled herself. She had to focus her energies on formulating a plan to get Rapunzel back to the tower.

Hearing a noise behind her, she swiftly ducked into the shadows. A group of angry palace guards raced past her and burst into the Snuggly Duckling.

Chapter 14

"**W**here's Rider?" the captain of the guards barked. "Where is he? I know he's in here somewhere." The captain surveyed the mangy crowd in the tavern. "Find him," he said to the other guards. "Turn this place upside down if you have to!"

Flynn grabbed Rapunzel, with Pascal still clinging to her hair, and ducked behind the counter. Peeking over the top, Flynn saw the palace guards bring in the Stabbington brothers. Their hands were in shackles. Then he saw Maximus clomp into the tavern and begin sniffing around. *That horse! How does that horse keep finding me?* Flynn wondered.

Someone reached down and grabbed Flynn and Rapunzel. Flynn cringed, thinking he was done for. But the thug lifted a hidden door in the floor, revealing a secret passageway.

"Go live your dream," the thug said sweetly.

"I will," Flynn told him, finding this turn of events bizarre but good. Really good!

"Your dream stinks," the thug bluntly told Flynn. Then he nodded at Rapunzel. "I was talking to her." Rapunzel smiled at the thug as Flynn entered the secret passageway.

"Are you coming, Blondie?" Flynn asked her.

Rapunzel looked into the dank tunnel and, after an encouraging smile from Pascal, followed Flynn. The door closed behind them, and Flynn and Rapunzel were suddenly gazing into a long, dimly lit passageway.

Inside the tavern, the royal guards continued their search.

Nobody paid attention to Maximus. The horse was used to it. But Maximus had picked up that scoundrel's scent, and he followed it until he saw a slight irregularity in the floorboards. He also saw Flynn's puny footprint. Maximus knocked his hoof against the floor, and a door swung open. *Aha!*

"A passage?" the captain said, coming up behind Maximus. "Come on, men. Let's go!" The horse charged into the passage, followed by the palace guards.

Before the captain entered the tunnel, he turned toward the Stabbington brothers.

"Conli, make sure those boys don't get away," the captain said to one of his guards. The guard nodded, and the captain disappeared into the tunnel.

"Does that hurt?" one of the Stabbingtons asked the man guarding them. The brothers were a full foot taller than he was. And they looked mean—meaner than any other prisoner that guard had seen.

"Does what hurt?" the guard replied nervously.

BAM! The brothers head-butted the guard so hard that he was slammed to the floor, unconscious. Grabbing a spear, the brothers used their brute strength to break their shackles.

"Play it safe?" one brother asked, pointing to the tavern door. "Or go get the crown?" Smiling evilly, they headed toward the tunnel.

They didn't care about safety. They wanted the precious crown.

Outside the tavern, Mother Gothel was still watching. If there was one thing Mother Gothel did well, it was watch. She knew that patience would always bring her the greatest reward. So she watched . . . and waited.

When she finally saw a thug stumble out the door of the Snuggly Duckling alone, Mother Gothel stepped from the shadows. "Excuse me, sir," she said, using her most caring voice. "I am desperately trying to find my daughter. Where does that tunnel let out?"

Inside the tunnel and happy to be making his escape, Flynn led the way. "You know," he said to Rapunzel awkwardly, embarrassed to have been rescued by a girl, "for the record, I had everything very under control."

"Oh." Rapunzel felt confused. "Okay."

"It was good of you to step in. So . . . thank you for that."

The tunnel was dark and cool. Flynn found a

lantern that cast a warm globe of light around them. They were moving swiftly now, but they still had a long way to go together.

"So, Flynn, where are you from?" Rapunzel asked.

But Flynn balked at the subject. After his humiliation in the tavern, he refused to reveal any personal information.

"So here is my question," he said. "If you want to see the lanterns so badly, why haven't you gone before?"

Rapunzel's eyes grew wide with fear. She faltered, "Uh . . . heh. Well . . ."

"No," Flynn insisted. "Seriously."

But even as he spoke, the cavern began to shake. Debris sifted down on their heads.

Rapunzel turned and saw Maximus charging down the tunnel toward them. The guardsmen were right behind him.

"Flynn!" she cried out.

One of the guards spotted them and shouted, "Rider!"

Flynn chose to respond to Rapunzel: "Run!"

Chapter 15

Flynn and Rapunzel dashed down the tunnel to the end of the passageway. Suddenly it opened out onto a vast cavern, which was dotted with huge stone pillars rising from the earth far below. Nearby was a rickety wooden dam holding back a vast amount of water. Flynn took one look behind him at the stampeding horse and guardsmen. He glanced down at the Stabbington brothers waiting for him at the base of the crevice.

Suddenly, he saw Rapunzel throw her hair across a large divide, lassoing a sturdy piece of stone. Tossing Flynn her frying pan, she swung across the crevice, landing safely on the outcrop.

Then the guardsmen were upon him.

"Ha!" Flynn shouted as he hit one sword after

another out of the guards' hands and knocked them unconscious. Rapunzel's pan was quite a weapon.

Then Flynn saw him: Maximus. The horse grasped a sword in his teeth. *CLANG!* Pan clashed against sword until Maximus knocked the pan right out of Flynn's hand. Just in the nick of time, Flynn heard Rapunzel call out to him. She tossed her long hair toward Flynn, and he grasped it. A fierce determination welled up inside her. She had done this before, many times, in the tower. It was like jumping from the rafters. Deftly, she looped her hair around an outcropping on her pillar and watched Flynn swing out over the canyon. She was aiming for him to glide all the way down to the bottom and make a soft landing.

As for Flynn, he felt as if he were flying! He had once again escaped Maximus and now was ready to make a landing! Then he saw the Stabbingtons. He had forgotten about them. They were standing there, right in his path, waiting with swords drawn. Flynn felt himself pulled upward as Rapunzel yanked on her hair.

He soared right over the Stabbingtons' heads! Flynn yelled, delighted—and then crashed right into a long water drain. The wooden contraption served as a funnel for excess water to leak out of the dam and wind its way to the base of the canyon. Flynn scrambled atop the wooden chute as Rapunzel prepared to swing down to the ground.

But a furious Maximus refused to give up. Rearing up on his hind legs, he knocked a large board from the dam above. It fell exactly as Maximus planned—making a bridge for him and the guards to run to the next pillar down, a bit closer to Flynn.

But the broken board had another effect: the rickety wooden dam loosened and cracked. Water began spurting through the dam's increasing number of crevices, threatening an explosive flood at any moment!

Flynn was terrified. The gigantic dam was about to burst, but he couldn't get to Rapunzel. And the Stabbingtons were right there, ready to attack both of them. Quickly, Rapunzel threw her hair again, watching it twirl and wrap perfectly around a sturdy rock. With her hair firmly anchored, she swung down toward the ground, slipping to a landing. She was unharmed, but the Stabbingtons were racing straight toward her!

Flynn jumped into the wooden drainage chute and slid down toward Rapunzel.

Dashing forward, Flynn tried to gauge where she might come to a stop. Then he saw it: she was on a collision course with the rocky floor of the cavern.

Flynn raced and dove. At the last possible moment, he caught her!

Chapter 16

The crash of the dam bursting was earth-shaking. Water roared into the cavern.

The powerful moving wall of water knocked down a pillar as Flynn ran. Dashing at top speed, he caught up with Rapunzel and Pascal. Flynn grabbed an armload of Rapunzel's hair as the two ran for cover. The Stabbingtons were washed away in a flood of water. An enormous pillar cracked and began to topple under the power of the rushing water. Rapunzel and Flynn had ten feet to get to the safety of a small shelter, a sort of cave—but the pillar was falling right toward them. Their legs pumping, Flynn and Rapunzel took one last mighty leap. The pillar crashed down just behind them as they ducked into the cave. They covered their heads as an avalanche of broken rocks showered down and blocked the entrance.

The palace guardsmen and Maximus were swept away in the rushing water outside.

Flynn and Rapunzel were safe for now, but the tunnel's entrance was blocked by the rubble from the fallen pillar. Flynn, Rapunzel, and little Pascal were now sealed inside a rocky cavern.

The sealed cavern did not protect them from the rushing water. Within minutes, Flynn and Rapunzel were waist deep in water—water that was rising quickly. Flynn dove down, searching for an exit. He hardly noticed the huge gash on his hand as he grasped for any opening among the jagged rocks.

"It's no use," he said, gasping, as he emerged from the dark water. "I can't see anything."

Rapunzel took a deep breath. She was about to dive underwater when Flynn took her wrist. "Hey, look," he said, "there's no point, Blondie. It's pitch-black down there."

Flynn and Rapunzel looked at each other helplessly. Having come so far together, they would die together in this little cave.

"This is all my fault," Rapunzel said. "Mother Gothel was right. I never should have done this. I'm so sorry, Flynn." Rapunzel couldn't help thinking of Mother Gothel's warnings about the world outside the tower, and yet . . . Mother Gothel had been wrong about some things. She had told Rapunzel that the tavern thugs and Flynn were evil, but the thugs had become her friends, and Flynn—

"Eugene," he said as he grasped Rapunzel's hand. It was a dying man's confession. "My real name's Eugene Fitzherbert. Someone might as well know."

After a moment of silence, Rapunzel blurted out her own secret: "I have magic hair that glows when I sing." She couldn't believe it— she had broken one of Mother Gothel's rules by telling Flynn about her hair!

"What?" Flynn wasn't sure he'd heard her correctly.

"I have magic hair that glows when I sing!" As she spoke, Rapunzel realized that her hair might help them find a way out of the cave.

Flynn stared at her speechlessly as she began to sing. Within moments, her hair started to glow, lighting up the cave.

Rapunzel took a deep breath and dove underwater, lighting their way. Following her, Flynn saw a small opening in the corner of the cave. He took her hand and they swam to it. Yanking at stones with all his energy, Flynn broke through at last.

The water burst through the opening, carrying Flynn and Rapunzel out into the river.

Coughing and gasping for air, Rapunzel, Pascal, and Flynn threw themselves onto the riverbank. Lying facedown, the three took a few moments just to breathe.

"I'm alive!" Rapunzel choked out.

Flynn looked at Pascal. Flynn was pale, and his eyes were wide with disbelief. He had done many daring things in his life, but he had never, ever experienced anything like this! "Her hair glows!" Flynn stifled a tiny shriek as he spoke to Pascal.

"I'm alive!" Rapunzel screamed joyfully, not even hearing Flynn.

"I didn't see that coming," Flynn desperately whispered to Pascal. The chameleon stared right back at him, unblinking. "The hair actually glows!"

"Eugene!" Rapunzel called out.

"Why does her hair glow?" Flynn asked Pascal, but the chameleon could only shrug.

"Eugene!" Rapunzel shouted, trying to get his attention.

"What?" Flynn shouted in reply. He was still in shock, trying to figure it all out. Rapunzel began dragging her hair out of the water. As she squeezed it dry, she stared at Flynn's injured hand. It looked terrible.

Rapunzel sighed. Flynn was freaked out by her. But she needed to help him. "It doesn't just glow," she added.

Flynn's jaw dropped. He looked at Pascal, who was staring at him with a very wide grin spreading impishly across his face. The chameleon knew that Flynn was in for an even bigger surprise.

Chapter 17

Mother Gothel's dagger had been very convincing to the thug she had met outside the Snuggly Duckling. He had told her exactly how to get to the exit from the tunnel into which Rapunzel and Flynn had escaped.

Having found her way to that very exit, Mother Gothel waited with her long dagger hidden in her cloak. She was ready to use it to get Rapunzel away from that thief Flynn Rider. But when the tunnel door finally opened, it wasn't Flynn Rider and Rapunzel who came out. It was those two criminals she'd seen in shackles at the tavern. Mother Gothel quickly ducked behind a tree.

"I'll kill him. I'll kill that Rider," the talking Stabbington said angrily to his brother. "We'll cut him off at the kingdom and get back the crown. Come on!"

"Or perhaps you want to stop acting like wild dogs chasing their tails and think for a moment?" Mother Gothel rasped from her hiding place. Her plans had suddenly changed.

The startled Stabbington brothers drew their swords. Mother Gothel fearlessly stepped out from behind the tree.

"There's no need for that." She tossed them the satchel she had found in the tower and watched as they removed the crown and smiled broadly. Mother Gothel would not fight these two men. She hoped they could help her, so she offered them the crown for free and tempted them with something better.

"Well, if that crown is all you want, then be on your way," she said. "I was going to offer you something worth one thousand times that single crown." The two brothers stared at her. "It would have made you rich beyond belief," Mother Gothel continued. "That wasn't even the best part." She paused, taking time to let out a hearty laugh. "Ah, well! *C'est la vie!*"

As Mother Gothel turned to leave, she heard a voice behind her. "What's the best part?"

Mother Gothel held up Flynn's WANTED poster and slyly goaded the boys: "What if it came with revenge on Flynn Rider?" The Stabbingtons were suddenly all ears. Mother Gothel smiled wickedly. With their help, she would get Rapunzel back and get rid of Flynn Rider once and for all.

At that same moment, along the banks of the river, Flynn and Rapunzel were sitting by a campfire, drying out. Rapunzel took Flynn's injured hand and began wrapping her hair around it. This was her gift, and she needed to use it to help Flynn.

Flynn looked at her quizzically as she covered his hand with her hair.

"Flynn. Please," Rapunzel said soothingly. "Just . . . don't . . . freak out."

Slowly, softly, she began to sing. Her hair began to glow. The long loops of hair that surrounded their campsite lit up the night.

Flynn gazed in amazement but stayed silent. Something was happening to his injured hand. He could feel it. The hair felt warm and soothing, as soft and sweet as Rapunzel's voice.

When she finished, she gently pulled her hair from Flynn's palm.

He looked at Pascal. The little chameleon signaled to him to look at his hand.

It was completely healed!

"Oh," Flynn said in a wavery voice, filled with dismay.

"Are you completely freaked out?" Rapunzel asked, dreading the response.

Flynn answered abruptly, "What? Me? Freaked out? No, not at all." The problem was—he *was* freaked out! He let out a little shriek—actually a thunderous scream. Then, controlling himself, he resumed: "So. That's pretty neat—what your hair does. How long has that been going on, exactly?"

"I don't know." Rapunzel sighed. But she did trust Flynn. It was time to tell him her story. "People tried to cut it once when I was younger. They wanted to take it themselves. But when it's cut, it loses its power. A gift like that? It has to be protected. That's why Mother never let me . . ." Rapunzel sighed again. Should she tell Flynn that she had never left the tower? "That's why I never left the . . ."

Finally understanding, Flynn finished her sentence. "You never left that tower." The revelation both shocked him and made him want to protect her. "And you're still going to go back?"

"No!" Rapunzel replied. Then she said, "Yes. Ughhhhh!" She buried her face in her hands. "It's complicated."

Quickly, she changed the subject. She wanted to know more about Flynn Rider. It turned out that Flynn was the richest, most powerful man in the world. He was a man who could do anything and go anywhere he wanted. He was a man in a book that Flynn—or rather, Eugene—had read every night when he was a child. Over time, Eugene had adopted the name as his own.

When he finished with his story, Flynn stood up and stretched. "I need to get some more firewood," he said. Promising to return soon, he wandered off into the pitch-black forest.

As Rapunzel felt the warmth of the fire enveloping her, she heard a darkly familiar voice behind her. Startled, she turned to face the cloaked and hooded visitor.

Chapter 18

Rapunzel gasped as she stared at the shadowed figure of Mother Gothel.

"Hello, dear," Mother Gothel said.

"What . . . what are you doing here?" Rapunzel said, fumbling for words. "I mean, how did you find me?"

Mother Gothel walked up to Rapunzel and gave her hug. "Oh, it was easy, really," she said. "I just listened for the sound of complete and utter betrayal and followed that."

Rapunzel tried to find a way to explain. She couldn't help feeling guilty.

"We're going home, Rapunzel," Mother Gothel commanded. "Now."

"You don't understand," Rapunzel said. "I've been on this incredible journey, and I've seen and learned so much! I even met someone."

"Yes. The wanted thief." Mother Gothel frowned with disgust.

"No, Mother, wait! I think he likes me."

"Likes you?" Mother Gothel said, scowling at Rapunzel. It was ridiculous for Rapunzel to think that this ruffian could be fond of her, the unworldly child! "This is why you should never have left!" Mother Gothel scoffed. "This whole romance that you've invented just proves that you're too naïve to be here. Why would he like you, really?"

Mother Gothel was mocking her, trying to unravel the trust she had put in Flynn.

Rapunzel had heard Mother Gothel's scornful dismissals before. She had even accepted them. But she no longer believed them the way she used to. Mother Gothel had lied to her throughout her life. Rapunzel knew Flynn liked her. She knew she had made friends in the outside world. But at the same time, her doubts remained, tickling the back of her mind. Maybe—maybe Flynn was just trying to be honorable, to keep up his side of their deal.

"Come, come," Mother Gothel said. "You know that I'm right." She tossed the crown to Rapunzel. She challenged Rapunzel to give it to Flynn and find out what he really wanted.

Rapunzel began to wonder: If she gave the crown to Flynn, would he stop being nice to her? Would he leave her alone and run away with his prized crown?

"No," Rapunzel said firmly.

The firelight flashed across Mother Gothel's face as it filled with rage. Rapunzel was doubting her own mother.

"Don't say I didn't warn you. Show him this." Mother Gothel gestured toward the crown. "Then see how much he likes you!"

"I will!" Rapunzel said defiantly. But seeing her mother move to leave, Rapunzel called out, "Mother, wait!"

Mother Gothel simply turned her back and disappeared into the dark forest.

Rapunzel sat in silence. Minutes ticked by, and Flynn returned.

Flynn began talking to her lightheartedly, but Rapunzel hardly heard a word.

"Hey, you okay?" Flynn asked, returning from the woods.

Rapunzel turned around. "Sorry, yes," she told him. "I was just, uh, lost in thought, I guess."

Flynn began to tend the fire. "So, I have a question," he said, still intrigued by Rapunzel and her amazing gifts. "Will your hair work if you sing about anything? Like, I don't know, if you sang a song about cupcakes?"

Rapunzel didn't answer him. She just stared up at a knot in the tree where she'd hidden the crown and the satchel. She had believed in Mother Gothel her entire life. But now that she knew Flynn, she felt lost. It was impossible to believe in them both.

Meanwhile, the Stabbington brothers were hiding in the woods with Mother Gothel. They wanted to grab Flynn, the crown, and the girl with the golden hair right then and there. But Mother Gothel held them back. "Patience, boys," she whispered. "Trust me, it's all going exactly to plan."

Chapter 19

As the sun rose over their little campsite, Flynn Rider was fast asleep. He didn't notice that Maximus had finally found him. Again. Maximus glared down at the sleeping man, wondering what he should do to him first.

The horse had galloped, swum, and scrambled up and down mountains, falling and picking himself up again, utterly exhausting himself trying to hunt Flynn down. And now the big horse had him. Maximus nipped at Flynn's sleeve as Flynn jumped to his feet.

Rapunzel awoke to a scream. The tenacious horse now had hold of Flynn's foot and was dragging him away!

Astonished at the sight, Rapunzel tried to help, grabbing Flynn's arms. Soon Rapunzel and Maximus were engaged in a tug-of-war with Flynn stretched between them.

"Don't worry, Blondie!" Flynn said, trying to sound as if he were in control. "I've got him right where I want him!"

"Give me him!" Rapunzel ordered Maximus. She and the horse were pulling Flynn in opposite directions when Flynn wiggled his foot out of the boot in Maximus's mouth. Flynn scrambled away. Maximus charged after him.

Rapunzel stepped in front of the horse. "Whoa, boy," she said softly. "Easy."

She took hold of the horse's bridle and whispered, "Easy, boy. Shhh. Whoa, boy."

Maximus looked at Rapunzel. She cared!

Peeking out from Rapunzel's hair, Pascal watched in awe as she tamed the horse.

"That's it," Rapunzel said sweetly. "Now sit." Maximus hesitated. But Rapunzel looked him in the eye and said again, "Sit."

This time Maximus sat. It felt good. He had been racing and hunting and sniffing and falling over cliffs for days now! Rapunzel smiled. "You're such a good boy," she said, patting the horse's neck. "Yes, you are. Now drop the boot."

The boot instantly fell from the horse's mouth. Rapunzel patted him gently. "Oh, look at you, all wet and tired. Are you tired from chasing this bad man all over the place?"

Maximus had always thought that women had a gentler touch than men when it came to caring for horses.

"Nobody appreciates you, do they?" she asked kindly.

Flynn was shocked. She was taking sides— the wrong side! "What? You're kidding me," he said, putting his boot back on.

But Rapunzel ignored Flynn and kept talking to the horse. "Yes, you are tired, and nobody appreciates you, do they? Do they?" The horse neighed, and Rapunzel nodded sympathetically.

"Oh, come on!" Flynn said impatiently. "He's a bad horse!"

Rapunzel just shrugged the comment off. "Oh, he's nothing but a big sweetheart," she said. She read the name printed on the horse's bridle and smiled. "Isn't that right, Maximus?"

Flynn rolled his eyes. "You've got to be

kidding me." Then he cringed just a bit. He wondered, *Am I actually jealous of a horse? Ugh!*

Rapunzel looked into the horse's big eyes and explained everything very sweetly to him. "Today is the biggest day of my life," she said. Maximus nodded. "And the thing is, I want you not to get Flynn arrested. Just for twenty-four hours, and then you can chase each other to your hearts' content. Okay?" Rapunzel paused. "And it's also my birthday—just so you know."

The horse whinnied and shook his big head as if to say everything was okay. But he was only doing this for Rapunzel.

Carefully, Rapunzel guided Maximus and Flynn together. She wanted them to shake hoof and hand in a truce. Man and horse glared at each other angrily. They could not stand each other.

The horse snorted and finally raised his hoof. Flynn grudgingly reached out to shake it. He was only doing this for Rapunzel.

"Oof!" Flynn felt the hoof bypass his hand and punch him in the gut. *So much for starting a truce the nice way,* Flynn thought.

It was the beginning of a perfect day, Rapunzel thought. And just when she was sure it couldn't get any better, the bells of the kingdom began to ring in the distance.

Rapunzel darted to the crest of a nearby hill, following the sound of the bells.

In front of her lay a kingdom that was more beautiful than anything she could ever have imagined. Bordered by a body of crystal-blue water, an elegant castle sparkled in the sun, flags flying from its many spires. A village of lovely stone and wood cottages and small bridges nestled at its base.

Rapunzel turned and smiled at Flynn. She couldn't wait. Today she would visit the kingdom—and later see those lights at last.

Chapter 20

Before long, Rapunzel and Flynn reached the kingdom's gates. Pascal rode atop Maximus's head, grasping his ears and using them as reins. The little chameleon felt as if it was the biggest day of his life, too! As they approached a bridge and a group of palace guards, Flynn worried that he might be recognized and arrested. But Maximus was determined to take care of everything.

Hoping Rapunzel would notice his cleverness, Maximus spied a boy up ahead holding an armful of small kingdom flags. Rapunzel stared at the flags. There was something familiar about the purple background with the golden sun at its center. But she couldn't quite figure out what it was that was tickling her memory.

Maximus went into action, hoisting the boy into Flynn's arms. With a mass of flags shielding Flynn's face, they easily walked past the guards. Maximus glanced proudly at Rapunzel.

"Good morning!" Rapunzel cheerfully greeted the guards.

And then, all at once, Rapunzel was inside the village. She could hardly contain her excitement. People crowded the streets, talking and shopping, hanging out their laundry and busily doing other chores and errands. Everywhere she looked, she saw the bustle of life and laughter. It was absolutely enchanting.

She could smell cakes and breads baking. Up ahead, she saw beautiful fabrics and baskets hanging in market stalls.

Rapunzel hurried forward. She wanted to absorb it all!

"Whoa!" she cried out, nearly falling flat on the ground. Flynn and Maximus were instantly by her side. People were stepping on her hair! Trying to move through a crowd with seventy feet of hair was definitely a new experience—

and also a bit of a problem.

Rapunzel spotted a solution nearby. A group of girls were braiding one another's hair. As soon as they saw Rapunzel, their eyes grew wide. They rushed to touch her magnificent hair. Then they began to braid . . . and braid . . . and braid.

When they proudly finished, Rapunzel's hair was elegantly bundled down her back, the end of the braid well above her ankles.

"Thank you," Rapunzel told the girls as she moved on with Flynn and Maximus. Giggling, the girls looked at Flynn's hair, too. They had secretly braided it with pretty bows!

Rapunzel raced into a dress shop and tried on a cream-colored gown. It felt so soft and velvety that she couldn't help twirling happily around. Flynn took one look and his heart almost stopped. Rapunzel was stunning.

They bought a dozen pastries, covered with pink icing. Rapunzel had never tasted anything so delicious! The sweet sugar melted on her tongue as she ate them all! Poor Flynn hardly got a bite, but he did enjoy watching Rapunzel.

They stopped in a bookstore. Rapunzel had seen only three books in her life—the three books that Mother Gothel had allowed into the tower. Rapunzel looked at the bookstore shelves filled with hundreds of books and eagerly began trying to read them all. She could not believe how much she was learning and experiencing! Flynn was right next to her the whole time, pulling books from the shelves, gathering them on the floor, sitting beside her as she tried to take them all in.

Suddenly the town crier called out from a stage at the center of the village: "It is time, good people! Gather around! Yes, come, gather around! Today we dance to celebrate our lost princess. It is a dance of hope, where partners start together, separate, and return to one another. Just as one day our princess will return to us."

As the man spoke, a mosaic depicting the King and Queen caught Rapunzel's eye. She couldn't help gazing at the picture of the royal couple holding their baby—a portrait from the time just before the Princess was stolen from them. For some reason, Rapunzel felt mesmerized by the emerald-green eyes of the Queen and the little lost princess wearing the crown. The Queen looked almost exactly like Rapunzel.

Suddenly the town crier said, "Let the dance begin!" Flynn and Rapunzel were caught up in the dancing crowd as everyone moved around the village square.

Flynn twirled Rapunzel in time to the music. They separated and danced with other partners. Then they came together again—and their eyes locked. And just when Rapunzel thought it couldn't be more magical, the town crier shouted, "To the boats!"

The entire, wonderful day had passed, and now night was falling. It was time to release the lanterns.

Chapter 21

Rapunzel gave Maximus a wave as Flynn guided her aboard a boat and rowed away from the docks.

"Where are we going?" Rapunzel asked him.

"Well, if it's the best day of your life," Flynn replied, "you might as well have the best seat in the house."

Rapunzel turned back toward the docks and saw the kingdom laid out before her. "Oh, this is perfect!" she exclaimed.

"Yep," Flynn said, feeling proud of how well the day had gone. "Now we just sit and wait," he told her, knowing that the best was yet to come. "So, are you excited?"

"I'm thinking that I'm terrified," Rapunzel replied, staring silently at the water.

"Why?" Flynn asked.

"I've been sitting at a window for eighteen years, looking out and dreaming about what this place might look like, what I might feel when those lanterns rise tonight," she told him. "What if it's not everything I dreamed it would be?"

Flynn smiled. "It will be."

"And what if it is?" Rapunzel asked, feeling overwhelmed by it all. "What do I do then?"

"That's the good part, I guess," Flynn said as they gazed at the kingdom together. "You get to go find a new dream."

From their balcony inside the palace courtyard, the King and Queen launched the first lantern.

Rapunzel was nervously tossing flower petals into the water when she saw the reflection of the lantern as it floated into the sky. Overwhelmed, she turned her head upwards. Thousands of lanterns followed the first, filling the sky! Rapunzel was so excited when she looked up that she ran along the side of the boat, almost tipping it over.

It was as if she and Flynn were floating in a sea of stars.

Then Rapunzel turned to Flynn and saw that he had a lantern in his hands. He had gotten it in the village and hidden it in the boat, waiting for this moment to surprise Rapunzel with the gift.

Rapunzel was so thrilled, she rushed to him and held the lantern. "I can't believe I'm really here!" she exclaimed. "I don't know what it is, but I feel like I belong here."

Reaching down, she grabbed Flynn's satchel. "I have something for you, too," she said, handing it to him. "I should have given it to you before. But I was just scared. And the thing is, I'm not scared anymore. You know what I mean?" She wanted Flynn to understand. She wanted to confess to him that Mother Gothel had always told her that people like Flynn were evil, but that now . . . now Rapunzel believed in Flynn.

"Yeah. Yeah, I do," Flynn said truthfully. He knew that the crown was still in that satchel, but it no longer meant that much to him.

Quickly, he turned back to Rapunzel. Holding the lantern together, they released it into the sky.

Then Flynn leaned in closer.

He stopped just short of kissing Rapunzel. He glanced over her shoulder. The Stabbington brothers were on the shore, waiting for him.

"Is everything, okay?" Rapunzel asked.

"Yes . . . yes, of course," Flynn said, not wanting to ruin the day for her. He started rowing back toward the shore to face the Stabbington brothers.

"I'm sorry," he said. "Everything's fine, but there's just something I have to take care of."

Rapunzel, their journey together, all of it had changed Flynn's view of the world. He wanted to make things right. He was in love with Rapunzel. He no longer wanted to be a thief, a lone highwayman always running away from everything.

Flynn landed the boat on the shore and leaped out. He told Rapunzel to wait for him.

Flynn searched the bushes and found one of the Stabbington brothers by himself. Flynn tossed the satchel down in front of him.

"There," he said as the crown fell out of the bag and onto the ground. "You got what you wanted. Now leave us alone. I never want to see you again." Flynn turned to leave.

"Holding out on us again, eh, Rider?" said the one Stabbington as his brother sneaked up behind Flynn.

"What?" Flynn was confused, but one thing was for sure: the Stabbington brothers were not just interested in the crown anymore.

Chapter 22

In a menacing tone, the Stabbington without the eye patch told Flynn everything that he and his brother had learned from wicked Mother Gothel. "We heard you found something. Something much more valuable than a crown." Both brothers looked in the direction of the boat where Rapunzel sat waiting.

Flynn cringed as he realized the brothers had somehow found out about Rapunzel's magic hair. Desperately, he began to fight.

A little while later, Rapunzel was relieved to see a man finally step from the bushes. "I was starting to think you ran off with the crown and left me!" she said with a laugh, thinking it was Flynn.

"He did," a rough voice answered. Rapunzel gasped. She wasn't looking at Flynn. And it wasn't just one man, but two—the Stabbington brothers.

"What?" Rapunzel said, confused and panicked. "No, he wouldn't."

"See for yourself!" the talking brother replied, pointing toward the water.

Rapunzel looked and saw Flynn standing at the helm of a small ship.

She called to him. But Flynn didn't call back or turn to look at her. Rapunzel was crushed.

The brutish men behind her laughed. "A fair trade: a crown for the girl with the magic hair," the one brother said. "How much do you think someone would pay to stay young and healthy forever?"

Rapunzel didn't understand. How could this be happening? Had Flynn betrayed her, trading her and her magical hair for that thing in his satchel—that crown, which would bring him some reward money?

"No. No, please. No!" Rapunzel shouted as the brothers approached. And then she ran. She ran as fast as she could into the darkness.

Sadly, the braid that had held her hair up all day had begun to unravel. It caught on a branch, holding Rapunzel back! Terrified, Rapunzel struggled to get free. From behind her, she heard a loud clatter and some thumps.

Rapunzel looked back warily.

"Oh, my precious girl!" Mother Gothel said, brimming with emotion. The Stabbington brothers lay at her feet, knocked unconscious.

"Mother?" Rapunzel gasped. Mother Gothel threw her arms around the girl. Rapunzel hugged Mother Gothel, too, and finally broke down and cried.

"Are you all right? Are you hurt? Did they hurt you?" Mother Gothel asked.

"No. I'm fine, but, Mother, how did you . . . ?"

Mother Gothel was wringing her hands. "I was so worried about you, dear! So I followed you. And I saw them attack you, and . . . Oh, my, let's go, before they come to."

Rapunzel paused and looked back toward Flynn. He was sailing farther and farther away.

"You were right, Mother," she said, nodding.

Her eyes were blank and her heart was numb. So Flynn was the liar. "I'll never leave you again." Rapunzel had never felt such deep sorrow in her entire life.

"I know, darling. I know," Mother Gothel said as she held Rapunzel tight. Mother Gothel's voice seemed sad and sympathetic, but a small smile curled at the corners of her mouth. The evil woman had planned the whole series of events. She had tricked the Stabbington brothers into helping her trap Flynn and tie him, unconscious, to the ship. She had promised them a girl with magical golden hair who would bring them great wealth. And then she had betrayed them, knocking them unconscious. It was all for the sake of another lie. Mother Gothel had to make Rapunzel believe, once again, that Mother Gothel was the only person in the world whom she could trust.

Out in the harbor, the ship was now moving toward the dock, but not because Flynn was steering it. The Stabbingtons had knocked him unconscious and lashed him to the mast.

Following Mother Gothel's instructions, the brothers had tied the crown tightly to Flynn's hand. They knew what would happen when the palace guards found the drifting ship. Flynn Rider would be going off to jail.

Flynn was still unconscious when the current slammed the small ship into the dock. Two nearby palace guards heard the wood splinter. They looked over and saw Flynn Rider, the man on the WANTED poster, standing at the ship's helm.

Chapter 23

Flynn was jolted awake just in time to see the palace guards running toward him. He looked around in confusion, having no idea how he had gotten on the ship.

Then he heard a palace guard say, "Look! The crown!" And Flynn remembered the Stabbington brothers. Flynn knew they must have set him up, but all he cared about was what had happened to Rapunzel.

"Rapunzel? Rapunzel!" Flynn shouted out desperately.

The only witness to the whole sequence of events was Maximus. He knew he was supposed to keep Flynn out of trouble for twenty-four hours, and he was not happy. He snorted angrily and followed as the guards hauled Flynn off to the palace jail. Then he galloped straight toward the gates of the kingdom. He had to find help.

While the guards were busy locking up Flynn, Mother Gothel led Rapunzel back to the tower.

Rapunzel went directly to her loft. Pascal still clung to her hair near her shoulder, hoping to help somehow. But Rapunzel was dazed by everything that had happened. She couldn't believe Flynn had taken the crown and left her. As she slumped at the edge of her bed, her hand strayed to her pocket, from which she pulled out a small kingdom flag—purple, with a gold sun on it. She stared at the flag and sighed, thinking of Flynn, the friendly thugs in the tavern, the people in the kingdom. What had gone wrong? Pascal heaved a sigh as well and turned blue, reflecting Rapunzel's sad mood.

Rapunzel looked at poor Pascal. At least she still had one friend. Playfully, she tossed the little flag at him. She wanted to see him turn a happy yellow again.

"Oh, come on," she said to him, as she always

did when he turned blue on her account. "It's not that bad."

Rapunzel looked at her painted wall. That sun seemed to be everywhere, showing up in bright spots on the painting. She could see them now. Rapunzel slowly focused more closely on her handiwork. The kingdom's sun fit into every small blank place on her mural. All these years, without realizing it, Rapunzel had been incorporating the outline of the golden sun in the empty spaces of the picture!

A flood of images suddenly filled Rapunzel's head. She recalled Flynn saying that the lights were floating lanterns that the kingdom sent up every year on the lost princess's birthday—*her* birthday. She remembered the mosaic of the royal family. The King and Queen were holding the lost princess. The Queen and the baby both had green eyes just like Rapunzel's. She remembered her reflection in the mirror when she placed the crown on her head.

As Rapunzel looked up at all those golden suns, everything fell into place. Rapunzel, at last, knew exactly who she was.

"Rapunzel?" Mother Gothel called up to her. But there was no answer. Mother Gothel, anxious to be on her way and put this whole nasty business behind them, slowly began to climb the stairs to Rapunzel's room.

"Rapunzel, what's going on up there? Are you all right?" she asked impatiently.

Mother Gothel's eyes grew wide when she saw Rapunzel standing above her on the stairs.

"I'm the lost princess," Rapunzel said softly.

Mother Gothel tried to dismiss it all. "Oh, please speak up, Rapunzel. You know I hate mumbling," she snapped, but Rapunzel saw the fear in the older woman's eyes.

"I am the lost princess, aren't I?" Rapunzel repeated loudly and clearly. "Did I mumble, Mother?"

Chapter 24

Mother Gothel froze. Her mind ran wild. Her secret was finally exposed. Desperately, she tried to regain control, saying brusquely, "Rapunzel, do you even hear yourself? Why would you ask such a ridiculous question?"

Rapunzel walked past Mother Gothel and went down the stairs. Mother Gothel had lied to her. She had been lying to her ever since she had stolen her away from her true parents.

"It was you!" Rapunzel said coldly. Now she was thinking of Flynn. Mother Gothel had set him up. "It was all you!"

"Everything I did was to protect you," Mother Gothel said, pleading with Rapunzel. "Where will you go?" she suddenly asked sharply. "He won't be there for you!"

Rapunzel turned and looked at her. "What did you do to him?" she demanded. She felt her heart swell, her love for Flynn giving her the courage to stand up to Mother Gothel at last.

"That criminal is to be hanged for his crimes," Mother Gothel said cruelly.

"No," Rapunzel murmured, horrified. "No."

Mother Gothel could see that Rapunzel was upset, and she moved closer to make the most of the opportunity.

"Now, now. It's all right," Mother Gothel said in her most soothing voice. She held out her arms as she always had. "All is as it should be."

"How could you do this? I love him," Rapunzel said.

Mother Gothel reached out to pat Rapunzel's head as if she were a small child. "I know you think you do, dear," she said in her silkiest, most soothing voice.

"No," Rapunzel said firmly as she grasped Mother Gothel's outstretched arm. "You were wrong about the world, Mother. And you were wrong about me. I am not stupid, and I am not small. And I will never let you use my hair again!" Rapunzel twisted Mother Gothel's arm and pushed her away. The older woman stumbled backward and crashed into her full-length mirror. The mirror shattered, its broken shards dropping to the floor. Rapunzel turned and defiantly walked away.

Mother Gothel glared at her. "Fine," the older woman said under her breath. She had given Rapunzel her chance to go back to the way things used to be. Now Mother Gothel would use stronger means to keep the girl with the golden hair imprisoned.

In the kingdom's jail, Flynn sat in his cell, wondering where Rapunzel was and whether she was hurt or in trouble. He blamed himself. If he hadn't stolen the crown, he never would have gotten mixed up with those Stabbington brothers.

"Let's get this over with, Rider," a jail guard announced as he unlocked the cell door. Flynn knew he was in trouble. After all, he had stolen the lost princess's crown. The punishment was death by hanging.

Still, he was more worried about Rapunzel. As two guards escorted him through the jail, Flynn spotted the Stabbingtons in one of the cells. Breaking free from the guards, he grabbed one of the brothers by the collar.

"How did you know about her? Tell me, NOW!" Flynn needed to know what had happened, how they had known about Rapunzel—where she was!

"It wasn't us. It was the old lady."

Flynn tightened his grip, but the guards rushed up and pulled him back roughly.

"Wait, wait!" Flynn shouted to the guards. "Wait! You don't understand, she's in trouble!" He didn't care that they were leading him to his death. He needed to save Rapunzel!

Suddenly he heard a ruckus outside. Flynn's jaw dropped. The thugs from the Snuggly Duckling had arrived! And they had come to break Flynn out of jail. Flynn didn't know how or why they had come, but he leaped at the opportunity.

Swinging his chains, he knocked over the

two guards. He and the thugs raced outside and headed toward the kingdom's gates. The thugs punched and smacked and wrestled the royal guards to the ground. Finally one of the thugs grabbed Flynn and put him on a wheelbarrow. Then, using the barrow as a seesaw, another thug jumped on the other end, launching Flynn into the air. He landed perfectly on Maximus's back. The horse snorted at Flynn. He hoped Flynn had finally noticed what an excellent horse he was. Maximus had galloped to find the thugs from the Snuggly Duckling and lead them to Flynn.

"Shut the gates! Shut the gates! Shut the gates!" the guards yelled. Maximus charged! The speedy horse zipped right through the gates as they slammed shut. Safely outside, Flynn and Maximus raced to save Rapunzel.

Chapter 25

"**R**apunzel!" Flynn yelled as he jumped off Maximus's back. No answer. "Rapunzel, let down your hair!" he yelled again, desperately hoping she was safe.

Swoosh! Rapunzel's long blond hair glided out of the window and down the tower. She was alive! Grasping her hair, Flynn climbed up the tower as fast as he could. At last, he made it to the window and hauled himself inside.

"Rapunzel, I thought I'd never see you again!" Flynn exclaimed. Then he stopped short and gasped. In the darkness, he saw the shards of a broken mirror on the floor—and heard the muffled sound of Rapunzel's voice. She was kneeling on the floor across from him. Mother Gothel had chained her to the wall and gagged her. Rapunzel's eyes were wide with fear as she struggled to warn him. . . . Then Flynn felt the sharp point of Mother Gothel's dagger against his back. He crumpled to the floor in pain.

Rapunzel cried out through the rags stuffed in her mouth. But Mother Gothel stared at her coldly and said, "Now look what you've done, Rapunzel. Oh, don't you worry, dear. Our secret will die with him."

Rapunzel could not speak, but now she understood: Mother Gothel intended to leave Flynn here to die!

Rapunzel needed to save him with her hair!

Mother Gothel unfastened Rapunzel's chains and dragged her toward the secret trapdoor in the floor. "And as for us, we are going where no will ever find you." Mother Gothel yanked Rapunzel, who was struggling against her with all her might.

"Rapunzel! Really!" Mother Gothel shouted. "Enough already! STOP FIGHTING ME!"

But Rapunzel did fight—as hard as she could—until the rags fell from her mouth.

"No!" Rapunzel cried out in defiance. "I

won't stop! For every minute, for the rest of my life, I will fight!" Rapunzel was stronger now, stronger than she ever had been. At last she knew the truth. She knew everything, and she understood everything clearly. "I will never stop trying to get away from you." She drew a deep breath, refusing to take her eyes off Mother Gothel. And she made her choice. "If you let me save him, I will go with you."

"No!" Flynn cried out. Rapunzel needed to be free from this woman. "No, Rapunzel!"

But Rapunzel kept her gaze on Mother Gothel. "I'll never run," Rapunzel promised. "I'll never try to escape. Just let me heal him. And you and I will be together. Forever. Just like you want." Rapunzel knew that her promise meant she would never see Flynn again, but at least she would know that he was alive, living outside in the beautiful world filled with wonderful, kind people. Her voice barely a whisper, she repeated, "Just let me heal him."

Mother Gothel's eyes narrowed for a moment before she let Rapunzel go.

Rapunzel ran to Flynn. He was still lying on

the floor, doubled over in pain.

"Rapunzel, no!" he said weakly. "I can't let you. . . ." His voice faded as he clutched a shard of the broken mirror. He would rather die than have the lovely, spirited Rapunzel live the rest of her life imprisoned in some secret tower with Mother Gothel.

Using his last ounce of strength, Flynn reached up and, in one swift motion, cut off Rapunzel's hair.

The long golden locks fell to the floor and turned brown, depleted of their magic. The short tufts of hair on Rapunzel's head also darkened.

"No! What have you done? NO!" Mother Gothel was clutching the brown hair that lay on the floor. The hair on her head turned white; her skin shriveled. Stumbling, she staggered across the room. She was aging rapidly, and quickly disintegrated into nothing more than a pile of dust. The evil woman was gone forever.

But Rapunzel was looking at Flynn. He was dying, and there was no magic left in her hair to save him! "Oh, no! Eugene! Don't go. Stay with me!" she sobbed. "Don't leave me. I can't do this without you."

"Hey," Flynn whispered with his last breaths. "You were my new dream."

"And you were mine, too." Rapunzel leaned toward Flynn as he closed his eyes.

Desperately, she began to sing. She wanted to bring forth some bit of magic from her shorn hair to save him. But the magic was gone with her hair.

Distraught, Rapunzel could not hold back her grief. She wept, cradling Flynn's limp body.

A single golden tear fell on his cheek.

Flynn stirred. Though she didn't know it, Rapunzel did have one last bit of magic left deep inside her, and it was contained in that single golden tear. Flynn's eyes fluttered open.

"Rapunzel!" he whispered.

"Eugene!"

Flynn was alive!

Chapter 26

Rapunzel returned to the kingdom with Flynn by her side. By now, everyone had heard about the return of the long-lost princess. (The thugs from the tavern were not exactly a quiet group, especially when it came to romance.)

Clutching Flynn's hand, Rapunzel followed a royal escort to the palace. Soon they entered the throne room.

Rapunzel heard a voice that seemed far away but actually was quite close. A royal guard was addressing her parents: "Your Majesties, this way. There she is!"

And then she saw them: the King and Queen. Rapunzel looked into their eyes. She knew. Their love seemed overwhelming, filling the room and Rapunzel's heart.

Flynn, too, felt overcome with emotion as he stood back and watched. Rapunzel, with her emerald-green eyes, looked exactly like her beautiful mother. As for the King, his eyes, aged by years of worrying about his daughter, suddenly brightened.

Unable to hold herself back, the Queen rushed to Rapunzel and held her tight. After a moment, the King joined them. Weeping with joy, the King and Queen knew, just as Rapunzel did. Their daughter, their precious child, had come home at last.

It did not take long for word to spread throughout the kingdom. A joyous celebration ensued. The people of the kingdom did what they had done for eighteen years, launching a thousand lanterns and then joining together in the palace courtyard to dance for—and this time with—their beloved princess.

And after that? They all lived happily ever after.